Shall We Dance?

by Ingrid Deringer

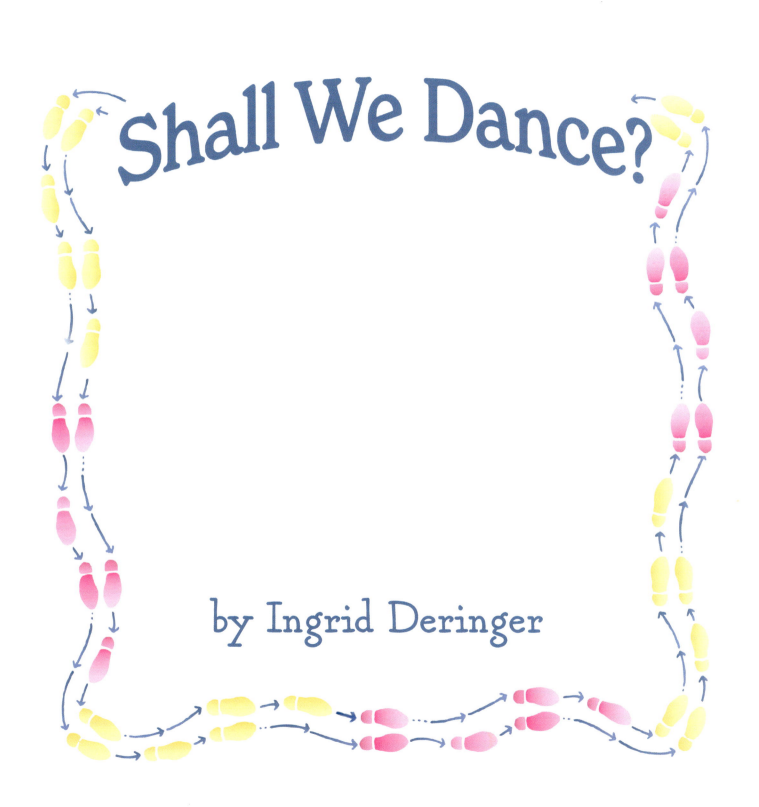

Copyright 2021 C. Ingrid Deringer

Dedication

To my mom, Piotta Deringer, who loved to sing and dance and taught my siblings and I all how to dance. And to my daughter Tania Elizabeth, the beautiful, talented and wonderful mother of Rio whose love of music has taken her Grandmother's legacy to new heights.

Thanks

Special thanks to my brother Karl Deringer, the best dancer in my family. When I dance with him my cheeks hurt from laughing and smiling so much. He also made sure I had the dance moves correct!

Thanks to my editor Claire Mulligan for her keen insight and on-going support in bringing my story to life and to Lynda Farrington Wilson for her whimsical illustrations that captured the love and joy of the story.

She loved rocking Baby Rio in her arms.
She loved walking outside with him in his snuggly.
She even loved changing his diapers!
But best of all, Grandma Ging Ging loved dancing with Baby Rio.

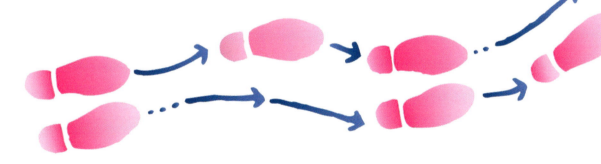

Whenever he cried or fussed, she held him cheek to cheek and asked, "Shall we dance a little?"

And at that baby Rio cooed and smiled.

Ging Ging lifted Rio up and they swayed back and forth, back and forth slowly, like a swing.

"This is called a Waltz," she told baby Rio.

One Two Three
One Two Three
One Two Three

And while they danced Ging Ging sang softly:

Dance when you get the chance, dear one
Laugh when you have a chance, dear one
You're young and your dreams are near
Love is what binds us together
And you have nothing to fear
Cause I am with you forever and ever

Rio grew to be two years old.

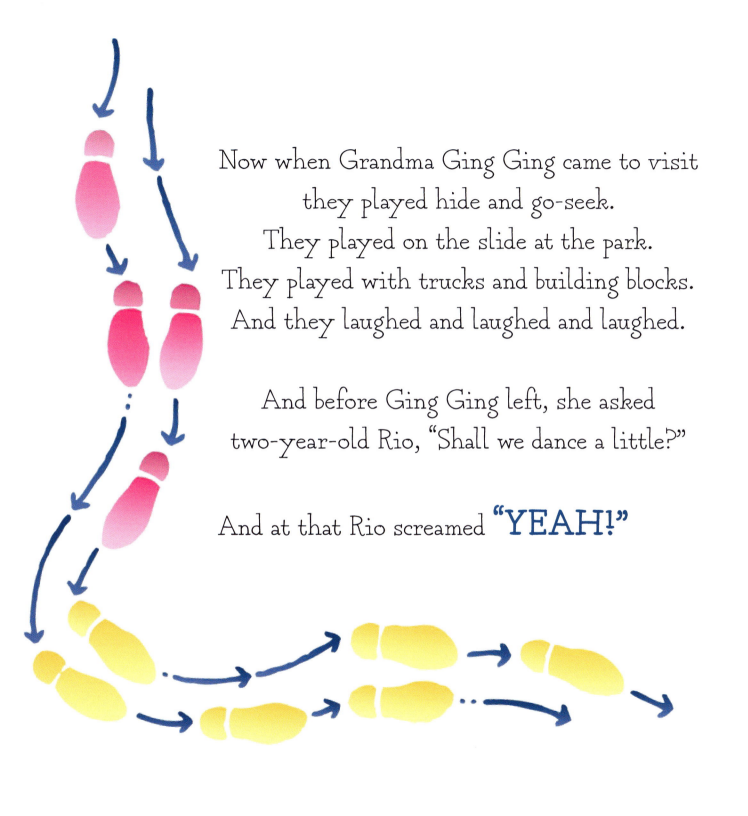

Now when Grandma Ging Ging came to visit they played hide and go-seek.
They played on the slide at the park.
They played with trucks and building blocks.
And they laughed and laughed and laughed.

And before Ging Ging left, she asked two-year-old Rio, "Shall we dance a little?"

And at that Rio screamed **"YEAH!"**

Ging Ging and Rio spun around and around like a spinning top, laughing their heads off!

"This is called a Polka Dance," she told Rio

One Two Three
One Two Three
One Two Three

And while they danced Ging Ging sang loudly:

Dance when you get the chance, dear one
Laugh when you have a chance, dear one
You're young and your dreams are near
Love is what binds us together
And you have nothing to fear
Cause I am with you forever and ever

Rio grew to be ten years old.

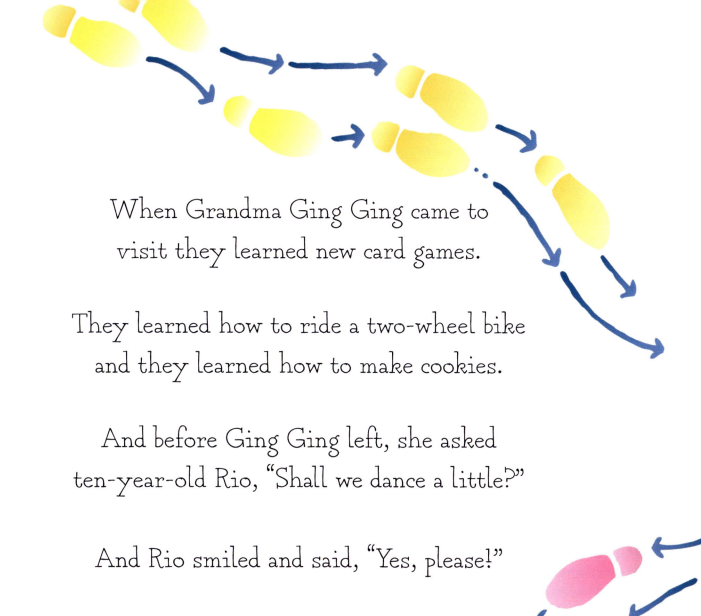

When Grandma Ging Ging came to visit they learned new card games.

They learned how to ride a two-wheel bike and they learned how to make cookies.

And before Ging Ging left, she asked ten-year-old Rio, "Shall we dance a little?"

And Rio smiled and said, "Yes, please!"

Ging Ging and Rio held hands and they waggled to and fro like honey bees, laughing their heads off!

"This is the called the Swing Dance," she told Rio.

One and two, rock step
One and two, rock step
One and two, rock step

And while they danced Ging Ging sang happily:

Dance when you get the chance, dear one
Laugh when you have a chance, dear one
You're young and your dreams are near
Love is what binds us together
And you have nothing to fear
Cause I am with you forever and ever

Rio grew to be sixteen years old.

Now when Grandma Ging Ging came to visit Rio he showed her how to play the drum kit.

And he showed her how to skateboard.

And he showed her how to make pizza from scratch.

And before Ging Ging left, she asked 16-year-old Rio, "Shall we dance a little?"

And in a deep voice, Rio said, "I would love to, Ging Ging."

Ging Ging held Rio's hand and they danced around and around like Spinner Dolphins.

"This is called the Two-Step Dance," she said.

Slow slow quick quick
Slow slow quick quick
Slow slow quick quick

And they laughed like crazy and as they danced Ging Ging sang:

Dance when you get the chance, dear one
Laugh when you have a chance, dear one
You're young and your dreams are near
Love is what binds us together
And you have nothing to fear
Cause I am with you forever and ever

Rio grew to be twenty-three years old.

Now, when Grandma Ging Ging came to visit Rio, they talked about his job.

They talked about his future.

And they talked as they walked in the park. Rio held onto Ging Ging so she wouldn't fall.

And Rio said: "I am getting married soon. Would you teach me how to Foxtrot so I can dance the Foxtrot at my wedding?"

And Ging Ging smiled a big smile and said, "I would be honoured."

When Rio got married, he asked his Grandma Ging Ging, "Shall we dance a little? And she said, "I would love to, my dear."

Rio held Ging Ging nice and close and they glided across the dance-floor like a pair of beautiful swans.

One two three four five six
One two three four five six
One two three four five six

And while they danced Ging Ging sweetly sang:

Dance when you get the chance, dear one
Laugh when you have a chance, dear one
You're young and your dreams are near
Love is what binds us together
And you have nothing to fear
Cause I am with you forever and ever

Ging Ging got older and older. One day she was a little old woman who could barely walk.

Now, when Rio came to visit Grandma Ging Ging, he asked if he could rub her feet with peppermint oil and brush her hair.

He asked if he could read her stories that he wrote. He asked if he could to take her out in her wheelchair to get some sunshine.

And before Rio left, he asked Ging Ging, "Shall we dance a little?"

And Ging Ging said, "Nothing would make me happier than to dance with you, but I am too old to dance now.

And Rio said, **"Oh, no, you aren't."**

Rio lifted Ging Ging up and he cradled her in his arms.
And he held her close so they were cheek to cheek.
And they waltzed, swaying back and forth,
back and forth slowly like a swing.

One two three
One two three
One two three

And as they danced Rio sang to his
Grandma Ging Ging ever so softly:

You danced when you had the chance, dear one
You laughed when you had the chance, dear one
You're old but your family is near
Love is what binds us together
And you have nothing to fear
Cause I am with you forever and ever